KAMALAPURAM DAYS

FOR HIS FURTHER EDUCATION SATHYA HAD TO GO TO KAMALAPURAM, A SMALL TOWN 210 KMS FROM PUTTAPARTHI. SATHYA'S ELDER BROTHER, SESHAMA RAJU, WAS WORKING AS A SCHOOL TEACHER AND STAYED IN HIS FATHER-IN-LAW'S HOUSE.

I AM SENDING SATHYA TO KAMALAPURAM FOR FURTHER EDUCATION AT THE BOARD MIDDLE SCHOOL.

GREAT HELP WITH THE HOUSEHOLD WORK.

SESHAMA RAJU'S WIFE SUSHEELA WAS VERY HAPPY.

IT WAS A BIG HOUSEHOLD AND THE YOUNG SATHYA WAS MADE TO DO MOST OF THE MENIAL HOUSEWORK.

SATHYA, GO TO THE CANAL AND BRING WATER IN THE BIG POT.

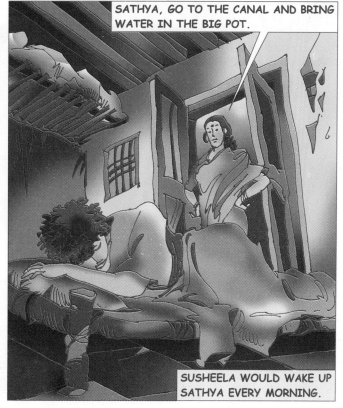

SUSHEELA WOULD WAKE UP SATHYA EVERY MORNING.

LITTLE SATHYA WOULD WALK TO THE CANAL THAT WAS QUITE FAR AWAY FROM THE HOUSE AND CARRY HOME THE HEAVY POT FILLED WITH WATER, REPEATING THIS TRIP IN THE EVENING.

SATHYA, I HAVE THE PORRIDGE READY, EAT IT AND GO TO SCHOOL.

POOR SATHYA, HE NEVER FINDS TIME TO STUDY AT HOME. HE IS MADE TO DO THE HOUSEWORK.

HIS FRIENDS WOULD FEEL SORRY FOR HIM

THE UNIFORMS

A FAIR WAS CONDUCTED EVERY YEAR AT PUSHPAGIRI NEAR KAMALAPURAM. THE FAIR IS BEING HELD THIS YEAR ALSO, WITH THE SAME FANFARE.

THE DRILL MASTER CALLED ALL THE STUDENTS.

ALL THE STUDENTS WILL GO TO THE FAIR TO VOLUNTEER SOCIAL SERVICE.

EACH STUDENT SHOULD WEAR A KHAKI SHIRT, KHAKI TROUSER WITH A BELT AND SHOULD CARRY A WHISTLE.

SATHYA, BEING THE CLASS LEADER, SHOULD GO TO THE FAIR WITHOUT FAIL.

SATHYA WAS WORRIED AND WALKED HOME SLOWLY THINKING WHAT TO DO.

SATHYA HAD ONLY ONE UNIFORM WITH HIM. EVERYDAY AFTER HE CAME HOME IN THE EVENING, HE WOULD WASH THE UNIFORM AND WEAR IT AGAIN NEXT DAY. THE UNIFORM WAS TORN IN FEW PLACES.

RAMESH, YOU KNOW I DO NOT HAVE A GOOD UNIFORM WITH ME. I WILL SAY I AM NOT WELL AND YOU BE THE LEADER.

RAMESH HESITATED AT FIRST, BUT ACCEPTED AFTER SATHYA INSISTED.

SURESH, ANOTHER CLOSE FRIEND OF SATHYA, LEARNT ABOUT SATHYA'S PLAN. SURESH'S FATHER WAS A RICH MAN AND WOULD BUY HIS SON ANYTHING HE WANTED.

I WANT TWO PAIRS OF KHAKI UNIFORMS TO GO TO THE FAIR.

I AM JUST LIKE YOUR BROTHER. IF YOU DO NOT TAKE THIS UNIFORM, I WILL DIE. I'LL BURN MYSELF OR KILL MYSELF IN SOME OTHER WAY.

SURESH PACKED ONE SET OF DRESS NEATLY AND WROTE A NOTE FOR SATHYA AND LEFT IT UNDER HIS DESK.

SATHYA SAW THE PACKET AND THE NOTE. HE TORE UP THE NOTE AND WROTE ANOTHER.

YES, YOU ARE LIKE MY BROTHER BUT FRIENDSHIP BASED ON MATERIAL BENEFITS WILL NOT LAST LONG. THERE SHOULD BE NO GIVE AND TAKE. FRIENDSHIP BASED ON PURE LOVE LASTS LONGER.

THE UNIFORMS

SATHYA RETURNED THE UNIFORM WITH THE NOTE. ALTHOUGH SURESH FELT BAD HE HAD NO CHOICE BUT TO TAKE BACK THE UNIFORM.

SATHYA WE WON'T GO UNLESS YOU COME. WE WON'T GO WITHOUT YOU.

EVEN IN THE SCHOOL THE STUDENTS TALKED ABOUT THE SAME THING. THEY EXERTED TREMENDOUS PRESSURE ON SATHYA TO GO TO THE FAIR.

DO NOT WORRY. I WILL COME.

ON THE DAY OF LEAVING FOR THE FAIR, ALL THE STUDENTS WANTED TO GO THERE IN A PROCESSION.

SUDDENLY, THEY WERE TOLD SATHYA WAS NOT WELL AND ALONG WITH THEIR TEACHER MEHBOOB KHAN, ALL OF THEM CAME TO SATHYA'S HOUSE.

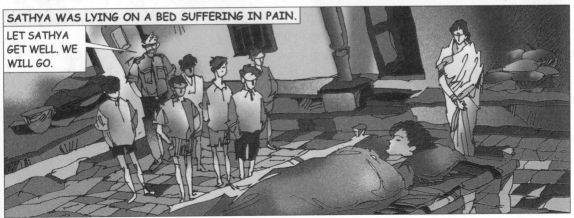

SATHYA WAS LYING ON A BED SUFFERING IN PAIN.

LET SATHYA GET WELL. WE WILL GO.

RELUCTANTLY ALL THE STUDENTS LEFT THE VILLAGE FOR THE FAIR.

SLOWLY SATHYA GOT UP FROM THE BED AND STARTED MOVING AROUND SAYING THAT HE WAS BEING RELIEVED OF PAIN.

EVEN THE FAMILY MEMBERS THOUGHT HE HAD REALLY BEEN IN PAIN!

PUSHPAGIRI FAIR

CHENNAKESHAVA SWAMY TEMPLE IN PUSHPAGIRI WHERE THE CATTLE FAIR TOOK PLACE WAS 11 KILOMETRES AWAY FROM KAMALAPURAM.

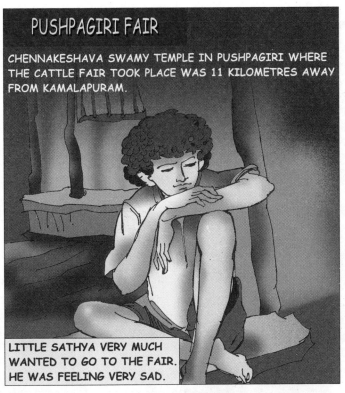

LITTLE SATHYA VERY MUCH WANTED TO GO TO THE FAIR. HE WAS FEELING VERY SAD.

EVERY STUDENT HAD PAID 12 ANNAS TO THE TEACHER, TEN ANNAS FOR THE BUS FARE AND TWO ANNAS FOR EXPENSES AT THE FAIR. WHERE WILL I GET THE MONEY?

MOREOVER A PAIR OF NEW KHAKI UNIFORMS IS ALSO REQUIRED! I DO NOT HAVE MONEY FOR BOTH.

SATHYA NEVER NEEDED TO READ BOOKS. HE COULD PASS THE EXAMINATIONS WITHOUT READING THE BOOKS. HIS TEXTBOOKS WERE AS GOOD AS NEW.

LET ME SELL THESE BOOKS AND GET SOME MONEY.

WILL YOU BUY MY BOOKS BECAUSE I NEED SOME MONEY?

I WILL BE PLEASED TO BUY THE BOOKS BUT I CAN ONLY PAY HALF THE COST.

HALF PRICE MEANS IT WORKS OUT TO 13 ANNAS. I DO NOT WANT EVEN THAT MUCH. IT IS ENOUGH IF I AM PAID FIVE ANNAS. I WILL GIVE YOU ALL THE BOOKS.

THE BOY WAS VERY HAPPY. HE WENT INSIDE AND BROUGHT FIVE ANNAS ALL IN SMALL COINS.

HOW SHALL I CARRY THEM?

HE TIED ALL THE MONEY IN A OLD PIECE OF CLOTH.

SATHYA CAME HOME HAPPY. BUT THE MOMENT HE ENTERED HOME THE WEAK CLOTH HOLDING THE COINS BURST AND ALL THE COINS FELL DOWN WITH A CLATTER.

SESHAMA RAJU'S MOTHER-IN-LAW SESHAMMA SAW THIS AND SHOUTED.

SATHYA HAS STOLEN THE MONEY FROM THE HOUSE!

NO MOTHER, I SOLD MY BOOKS AND GOT THE MONEY.

HE CALLED THE BOY AND SHOWED HIM TO HER.

SESHAMMA WOULD NOT BELIEVE THIS STORY. SHE BEAT BOTH THE BOYS, TOOK AWAY THE MONEY AND SENT THEM OUTSIDE.

IF I STAND OUTSIDE FOR MUCH LONGER PEOPLE WILL ASK WHY I AM HERE. I DO NOT WANT FAMILY PRESTIGE TO BE BROUGHT DOWN.

IT WAS ALREADY NIGHT. THE MOONLIT SKY WAS SOOTHING. WITHOUT HESITATION LITTLE SATHYA STARTED WALKING THE ELEVEN KILOMETRES.

SATHYA, WHY ARE YOU WALKING ALONE? COME WITH US. WE WILL GO TOGETHER.

BUT THE ELEVEN KILOMETRES WALK WAS TOO TIRING FOR LITTLE SATHYA. HE WAS EXHAUSTED BY THE TIME HE REACHED THE FAIR AT DAWN.

THE BOYS WERE ALREADY IN UNIFORM WHISTLING AND MOVING AROUND.

SATHYA FOUND ONE ANNA AND A PACKET OF *BEEDI** LYING IN FRONT OF HIM. HE TRIED TO FIND OUT IF IT BELONGED TO ANYONE.

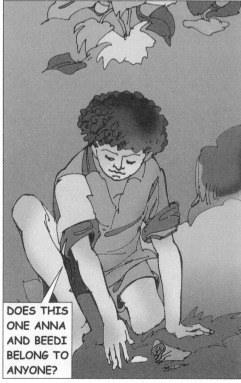

DOES THIS ONE ANNA AND BEEDI BELONG TO ANYONE?

*BEEDI: AN INDIAN FORM OF CIGARETTE

SATHYA TOOK THE ANNA AND BURIED THE BEEDI IN SAND.

A FEW PEOPLE WERE GAMBLING. SATHYA WANTED TO PLAY AND MAKE SOME MONEY.

THEN HE COMMITTED THE ONLY MISTAKE HE EVER COMMITTED IN HIS LIFE!

PLEASE ALLOW ME TO PLAY WITH YOU.

SATHYA ARRANGED EVERYTHING AND SLEPT. HE SLEPT VERY SOUNDLY AS HE WAS SO TIRED FROM THE OVERNIGHT WALK AND SPENDING THE WHOLE DAY IN THE HOT SUN.

WHEN HE WOKE UP IN THE MORNING HE FOUND THE MONEY MISSING! SOMEONE WHO HAD WATCHED SATHYA HIDING THE MONEY, MADE AWAY WITH IT WHEN SATHYA WAS ASLEEP.

SATHYA SPENT THE NEXT THREE DAYS WITHOUT ANY FOOD.

WHY YOU ARE NOT EATING ANYTHING, SATHYA?

AFTER THE FAIR

SATHYA RETURNED FROM THE FAIR AFTER TEN DAYS.

SESHAMA RAJU WAS ANGRY.

WHY DID YOU LEAVE FOR SO MANY DAYS? WHO WILL DO THE HOUSEWORK?

PEDDA VENKAMA RAJU CAME TO KNOW OF THIS. THE DISTRAUGHT FATHER CAME IMMEDIATELY TO KAMALAPURAM.

TEARS ROLLED FROM HIS EYES AFTER HE SAW THE PLIGHT OF HIS YOUNG SON.

COME, WE ARE GOING BACK TO PUTTAPARTHI IMMEDIATELY.

IT IS ALRIGHT FATHER; DO NOT WORRY NOW.

NO, YOU SHOULD COME AWAY IMMEDIATELY.

IT IS IMPROPER TO GO AWAY SUDDENLY LIKE THIS. I WILL BE HERE FOR ANOTHER COUPLE OF DAYS AND THEN I SHALL COME.

ALRIGHT, YOU COME BACK AS SOON AS POSSIBLE. DO YOU REQUIRE ANYTHING?

NO FATHER, I HAVE EVERYTHING.

PUBLICITY FOR MEDICINES

MEHBOOB KHAN, THE TEACHER, KNEW SATHYA'S DIVINITY AND LOVED HIM VERY MUCH.

SATHYA I HAVE BROUGHT SWEETS. IT HAS BEEN PREPARED IN A CLEANSED ATMOSPHERE. PLEASE EAT IT.

SATHYA SHOULD TAKE THE SWEET FIRST. ONLY THEN I WILL TAKE MY FOOD.

KOTTE SUBBANNA WAS A PROVISION SELLER IN KAMALAPURAM. ALONG WITH PROVISIONS HE WAS SELLING AYURVEDIC MEDICINES ALSO.

HOW CAN I MAKE MORE PEOPLE KNOW ABOUT MY PRODUCTS, SO THAT SALES WILL INCREASE?

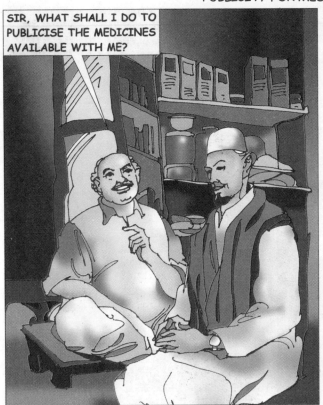

SIR, WHAT SHALL I DO TO PUBLICISE THE MEDICINES AVAILABLE WITH ME?

PLEASE DO NOT WORRY. SATHYA CAN WRITE BEAUTIFUL JINGLES FOR THE MEDICINES.

SATHYA WAS CALLED TO HELP! HE INSTANTLY CREATED BEAUTIFUL JINGLES FOR THE MEDICINES.

SING THOSE JINGLES AND GO AROUND THE VILLAGE. I WILL GIVE ALL OF YOU MONEY.

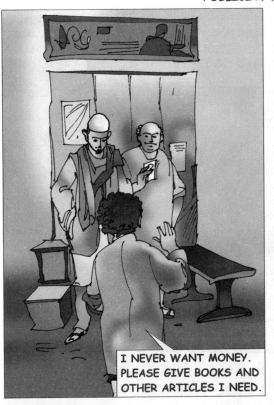

I NEVER WANT MONEY. PLEASE GIVE BOOKS AND OTHER ARTICLES I NEED.

AT THAT TIME A NEW MEDICINE BY NAME BALA BHASKARA CAME. SATHYA WROTE A POEM FOR THIS.
'WE HAVE FOUND BALA BHASKARA!'
COME, COME, OH BOYS!
ILLNESSES OF ALL SORTS,
PAINS AND SWOLLEN HANDS,
GOOD FOR ALL TROUBLES,
DISEASES OF WORST TYPE.
COME, COME, OH BOYS!
IF YOU ASK,
WHERE TO GET IT?
EVERYONE KNOWS IT!
LOOK! LOOK HERE
AT KOTTE SUBBANNA'S SHOP!
COME, COME OH BOYS!
PANDIT T. GOPALACHARY'S PRECIOUS TONIC!
COME, COME, OH BOYS!

AFTER THIS PUBLICITY THROUGH JINGLES THE SALES OF MEDICINES HAVE GONE UP CONSIDERABLY.

SATHYA! PLEASE WRITE JINGLES FOR US.

OTHER SHOP OWNERS ALSO STARTED APPROACHING SATHYA.

SATHYA WAS VERY PLEASED WITH THIS NEW ROLE. HE ENJOYED WRITING JINGLES.

ROCKING CHAIR

ONE DAY SATHYA WAS SITTING ON THE ROCKING CHAIR ROCKING HIMSELF BACK AND FORTH. HE REALLY ENJOYED DOING IT.

SESHAMA RAJU'S BROTHER-IN-LAW SUBBA RAJU ENTERED THE ROOM. SEEING RAJU ON THE ROCKING CHAIR HE BECAME ANGRY.

ARE YOU A PRINCE THAT YOU WANT A ROCKING CHAIR?

YOU DO NOT UNDERSTAND NOW, WHO I REALLY AM. YOU SHALL SEE IN TIME, WHETHER I AM A PRINCE OR SOMETHING BIGGER THAN THAT.

SUBBA RAJU PROTESTED, BUT SESHAMA RAJU DEFUSED THE SITUATION.

HEADMAN'S PREDICAMENT

SESHAMA RAJU COULD NOT TOLERATE THE POPULARITY OF SATHYA. HE WAS SENT BACK TO PUTTAPARTHI.

AFTER HIS RETURN TO PUTTAPARTHI, SATHYA CONTINUED WRITING POEMS.

THE KARNAM OF PUTTAPARTHI WAS A WEALTHY MAN, WITH TWO WIVES.

THE KARNAM IS WASTING HIS MONEY IN MANY BAD WAYS. BEING A HEADMAN HE SHOULD NOT DO THAT.

SATHYA WOULD COMPOSE SONGS. THE BOYS WOULD GO TO THE KARNAM'S HOUSE, STANDING IN FRONT OF THE GATE THEY WOULD SING SONGS DISCOURAGING HIM FROM DOING BAD THINGS.

WE SHOULD MAKE THE KARNAM REALIZE HIS MISTAKE AND LEAD A PROPER LIFE.

DO NOT GO TO THE HOUSES OF PROSTITUTES. DO NOT SPEND YOUR TIME AND MONEY WITH PROSTITUTES. PEOPLE WITH HONOUR WILL NOT TOUCH YOU. THE ELDERS WILL NOT LET YOU COME ANYWHERE NEAR THEM.

IN FACT THE LADIES ARE IN SUCH A FORM THAT WE CANNOT EVEN DESCRIBE THEM. WE CANNOT TALK HONOURABLY ABOUT THEIR DRESS, OR ABOUT THEIR APPEARANCE.

THE HEADMAN HAD GROWN A MUSTACHE, CALLED A HITLER'S MUSTACHE AT THAT TIME WHICH HAS A LITTLE BIT ON THE RIGHT SIDE AND LITTLE BIT ON THE LEFT SIDE OF THE NOSE. CHILDREN RIDICULED THAT ALSO.

THE KARNAM HAS REMOVED HIS HITLER'S MUSTACHE!

THE HEADMAN GOT ANNOYED OF ALL THIS AND COMPLAINED TO PEDDA VENKAMA RAJU.

SATHYA IS MAKING MY LIFE MISERABLE. THIS IS NOT CORRECT. PLEASE SILENCE HIM.

SATHYA PLEADED INNOCENCE.

NO FATHER, I DID NOT DO ANYTHING. YOU CAN ASK THE BOYS. I WAS NEVER PART OF ANY SINGING GROUP.

SONGS FOR FREEDOM FIGHT

SATHYA'S CAPACITY FOR COMPOSING POEMS TO SUIT ANY SITUATION SPREAD TO NEIGHBOURING BUKKAPATNAM AS WELL.

DURING THOSE DAYS THE STRUGGLE FOR INDIA'S INDEPENDENCE WAS GOING ON FIERCELY. MEETINGS WERE BEING HELD EVERY WHERE URGING FOR INDEPENDENCE. POLICE USED TO COME AND BREAK UP THE MEETINGS.

WRITE POEMS DESCRIBING THE PRESENT SITUATION. WE WILL SING THEM IN MEETINGS IN BUKKAPATNAM.

SATHYA, PLEASE COME WITH US. WE WILL PUT YOUR DRAMATIC TALENTS TO GOOD USE.

SATHYA COMPOSED POEMS AND WENT TO BUKKAPATNAM ALONG WITH THE CONGRESSMEN.

SATHYA WILL BE DRESSED LIKE A GIRL AND HE WILL SING LULLABIES TO THE DOLL.

CONSTRUCT A JHULA. LET SATHYA SIT IN THE JHULA HOLDING A RUBBER DOLL AND SING LULLABIES.

DO NOT CRY BABY. IF YOU CRY AND SHOW YOU CANNOT BE CHEERFUL, THEY WILL NOT CALL YOU A WORTHY CITIZEN, A WORTHY SON OF BHARAT.

ARE YOU CRYING BECAUSE THERE IS NO UNITY IN OUR COUNTRY? DON'T CRY. THERE WILL BE A TIME WHEN ALL OF US WILL BE UNITED AND WILL BE ABLE TO PRESENT A UNITED PICTURE. THERE IS A REMEDY. DO NOT CRY.

WHAT A BEAUTIFUL SONG! IT IS REALLY THRILLING.

THEY FORGOT THEIR DUTY AND STARTED CLAPPING ALONG WITH THE CROWD AND JOINED THE CHORUS.

THE BRITISH OFFICERS STARTED LIKING THE SINGING THOUGH THEY DID NOT UNDERSTAND *TELUGU**. THEY ALSO STARTED CLAPPING AND JOINED THE CROWD IN ENJOYING THE MUSIC.

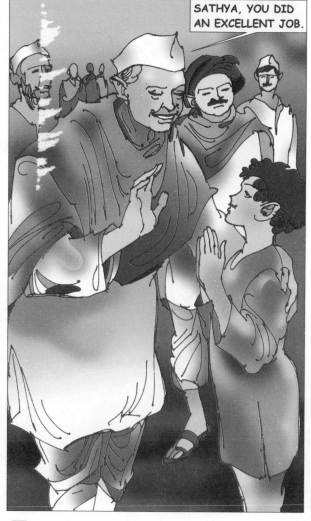

*TELUGU:REGIONAL LANGUAGE OF ANDHRA PRADESH